This Book belongs to

Princess Pistachio
Treasury

Praise for Princess Pistachio

"A playful and entertaining take on children's perennial questions surrounding ideas of personhood, family and community."
—*Kirkus* ★ **Starred Review**

"Young readers transitioning to chapter books will be enthralled by Pistachio and her big personality and imagination."
—*School Library Journal*

"Sometimes charming and sometimes funny, the story is as satisfying as its protagonist's name: Pistachio Shoelace."—*Booklist*

Praise for Princess Pistachio and the Pest

"In four breathless, fast-paced chapters, Gay once again weaves a frantically funny tale with deliciously named characters….Long live Princess Pistachio."—*Kirkus* ★ **Starred Review**

"This entertaining transitional reader is perfectly suited for children ready to try chapter books….Fans of other high-spirited girl characters like Junie B. Jones and Clementine will fall in love with Princess Pistachio."—*School Library Journal*

"[L]ively ink-and-watercolor illustrations brighten every page."
—*Booklist*

Praise for Princess Pistachio and Maurice
the Magnificent

"Irrepressible Princess Pistachio is back in all her enthusiastic glory….Gay's easy, breezy syntax is wonderfully descriptive even as it skillfully addresses life lessons about friendship, self-involvement, and forgiveness….Breathless, laugh-out-loud fun."
—*Kirkus* ★ **Starred Review**

"This lighthearted story about a young girl and her lazy dog will entice young readers who are venturing into chapter books….The child appeal of this tale will keep independent readers chuckling and wanting more."—*School Library Journal*

Princess Pistachio
Treasury

Marie-Louise Gay

pajamapress

First published in Canada and the United States in 2018
Text and illustrations copyright © 2018 Marie-Louise Gay
This edition copyright © 2018 Pajama Press Inc.

10 9 8 7 6 5 4 3 2 1

The publisher gratefully acknowledges the support of the Canada Council for the Arts and the
Ontario Arts Council for its publishing program. We acknowledge the financial support of the
Government of Canada through the Canada Book Fund (CBF) for our publishing activities.

Library and Archives Canada Cataloguing in Publication

Gay, Marie-Louise [Works. Selections. English]   Princess Pistachio treasury / Marie-
Louise Gay.
Princess Pistachio and Princess and the pest translated by Jacob Homel. Contents: Princess
Pistachio -- Princess Pistachio and the pest -- Princess Pistachio and Maurice the
magnificent. ISBN 978-1-77278-048-2 (hardcover)

        I. Homel, Jacob, 1987-, translator II. Gay, Marie-Louise. Malheurs de
princesse Pistache. English. III. Gay, Marie-Louise. Princesse Pistache. English. IV.
Gay, Marie-Louise. Princess Pistachio. V. Gay, Marie-Louise. Princess Pistachio and
the pest. VI. Gay, Marie-Louise. Princess Pistachio and Maurice the magnificent. VII. Title.

PS8563.A868A2 2018   jC843'.54
C2018-901648-5

Publisher Cataloging-in-Publication Data (U.S.)

Names: Gay, Marie-Louise, author.
Title: Princess Pistachio Treasury / Marie-Louise Gay.
Description: Toronto, Ontario, Canada: Pajama Press, 2018. | Summary: "A collection
for early readers of three illustrated stories about the impulsive and imaginative Pistachio
Shoelace: Princess Pistachio, in which she believes she is a kidnapped princess; Princess
Pistachio and the Pest, in which she must watch her troublemaking baby sister; and Princess
Pistachio and Maurice the Magnificent, in which her dog's starring role in a play leads to
fame and jealousy" — Provided by publisher.
Identifiers: ISBN 978-1-77278-048-2 (hardcover)
Subjects: LCSH: Dogs – Juvenile fiction. | Sisters – Juvenile fiction. | BISAC: JUVENILE
FICTION / Readers / Intermediate. | JUVENILE FICTION / Humorous Stories.
Classification: LCC PZ7.G39Pri |DDC [F] – dc23
Original art created with India ink, watercolor, ink, and colored pencils

Cover and book design—Rebecca Bender

Manufactured by Qualibre Inc./Print Plus
Printed in China

Pajama Press Inc.
181 Carlaw Ave. Suite 251 Toronto, Ontario Canada, M4M 2S1

Distributed in Canada by UTP Distribution
5201 Dufferin Street Toronto, Ontario Canada, M3H 5T8

Distributed in the U.S. by Ingram Publisher Services
1 Ingram Blvd. La Vergne, TN 37086, USA

Princess Pistachio

Translated by Jacob Homel

To Princess Élisa of Quissac
and to her big brother,
the knight Florian.

• Chapter 1 •
A Real Princess!

Happy birthday, my little princess!

Pistachio can't believe her eyes! She reads and rereads the card that came with the present she found under her bed.

Happy birthday, my little princess! The words dance before her eyes.

"Could it be?" Pistachio thinks.

"Might it be?" Pistachio hopes.

Her heart beats like a drum.

Pistachio unties the ribbon and rips off the paper. A golden crown. A crown for a princess!

"I knew it," Pistachio whispers. "I have always known it! I *am* a princess. A *real* princess!"

All her life, Pistachio believed that her real parents were the king and queen of

a magnificent kingdom. She had found the kingdom on her map of the world. A golden island in the middle of the Indian Ocean—Papua!

The king and queen of Papua adored their little princess. They gave her nothing but chocolates and chestnut ice cream to eat. They dressed her in the finest silks and most delicate ostrich feathers.

Every day, the king and queen showered her with presents—silver skates, invisible kites, a parrot that spoke five languages, and a piano-playing monkey. A thousand and one presents, each one more wonderful than the one before.

But one day, a ghastly witch, green with envy, stole their precious princess. The witch abandoned her on the other side of the world, at 23 Maple Street, with Mr. and Mrs. Shoelace, her adoptive parents. Ever since that terrible day, the king and queen of Papua had desperately searched for her.

"They have found me at last!"
Pistachio sings as she waltzes with her
dog around the room. "They will be
here any day now, to bring me back to
our kingdom. Me, Princess Pistachio of
Papua! Hurray!"

That evening at the dinner table, Pistachio breaks the news to her family. She stands on her chair and proclaims, "I know the whole truth now. From this day forth, you shall call me Princess Pistachio."

Pistachio's mother tries to get Penny to finish another spoonful of creamed spinach. Pistachio's little sister wiggles about like a sea worm and refuses to open her mouth.

"Well." Pistachio's mother sounds a little tired. "How lucky I am to be the mother of a princess."

Penny opens her mouth wide and sprays creamed spinach across the kitchen. "Penny pwincess too!"

The kitchen looks like a Martian battlefield. Spinach runs down the yellow walls, the white tablecloth, and Pistachio's magnificent pink princess dress. Even the dog is a lovely shade of green.

"You are…DISGUSTING!" shouts Princess Pistachio. "You could never be a princess! Besides, you are not even my sister!"

Penny begins to wail. Her face is as red as a beet. It looks quite nice next to the spinachy green.

"Enough!" her father says. "Stop teasing your sister, Pistachio."

"PRINCESS Pistachio," she replies.

"*Miss* Princess Pistachio," her father says, "would you be so kind as to sit down and eat your spinach?"

Princess Pistachio pouts in distaste.

"Princesses," she says, "never eat spinach."

"Princesses," her father replies, "always eat their spinach, or they can't have any dessert."

"I don't care about your crummy dessert!" Pistachio declares as she leaves the kitchen like a real princess: her head held high, her back straight, walking gracefully around the green puddles of spinach.

· Chapter 2 ·
An Angry Princess

The next morning, Pistachio's mother asks her to look after Penny in the garden.

"Can't you see I have other things to do?" Pistachio replies. "Besides, princesses *never* look after smelly babies."

"Princesses," her mother says, "*always* obey their mothers, or they go without television for a week."

"My real mother would never deny me anything," Pistachio mutters.

She sighs and looks at Penny out of the corner of her eye.

Penny immediately sticks a mud pie on her head like a crown and hollers, "I want to pway pwincess!"

Pistachio sticks out her tongue and turns her back to her little sister. She adjusts her golden crown and slips on her white gloves. Now she is ready for her triumphant tour of the garden.

Princess Pistachio walks with small, delicate steps, like a preening peacock. With a proud smile, she greets the birds on the clothesline. With a tiny nod of her head, she accepts the cheers from a crowd of fawning tulips. Finally, she bows her head and curtsies gracefully before the dog.

"Your Highness," she murmurs. "I am Princess Pistachio of Papua, at your service!"

The dog scratches his ear and yawns hard enough to unhinge his jaw.

Princess Pistachio sighs, again.

Suddenly, she hears a terrible cry.
She looks over the fence and sees two
dueling knights. Princess Pistachio is
horrified: they must be fighting out of
love for her!

"I am going to kill you dead, camel
head!" Gabriel shouts. His sword tears
through the air like lightning.

Jacob dodges the attack. "Missed me
again, clucking hen!"

"Stop! I beg of you!" Princess
Pistachio cries out.

Surprised, Gabriel and Jacob tumble
to the ground.

"Brave knights, I beg of you!" Princess
Pistachio beseeches. "The last thing
I wish is for one of you to die out of
devotion to me, Princess Pistachio of—"

The two boys look at each other, then
burst out laughing.

"Princess?" Gabriel sniggers. "Even an ugly old toad would want nothing to do with you!"

"To die for a mustachioed pistachi-toad! Ugh!" Jacob cries out.

They run away laughing like monkeys.

"Brutes! Peasants!" Pistachio screams. "I'll feed you to the lions!"

"Eat, dog, eat!" Penny shrieks from behind her.

Princess Pistachio turns around.
Penny is trying to feed tulips to the dog.
Her mother's precious yellow tulips.

The dog looks green.

Pistachio sees red.

She roars, "Penny, you bird brain!"

Penny wails and turns purple.

• Chapter 3 •
A Princess at School

On Monday morning, Princess
Pistachio's mother shakes her awake.

"Princesses do not go to school,"
Pistachio mutters and hides under the
covers.

"Oh, yes they do!" her mother replies.

"Princesses never get out of bed
before noon," Princess Pistachio
mumbles as she puts the pillow over her
head.

"Oh, yes they do!"
her mother insists.

"Princesses never—"

"Do you want me to turn into a horrible witch?" her mother asks. "Or a dragon?"

In a heartbeat, Pistachio jumps out of bed.

Pistachio smiles as she hurries to school. "My friends will be so impressed. I am sure they have never seen a real princess."

Indeed, Princess Pistachio makes quite an impression as she enters the

classroom. Her golden crown sparkles under the neon lights. Her princess gown trails elegantly behind her. Her classmates' eyes are as wide as saucers. Even Mrs. Trumpethead seems at a loss for words.

Princess Pistachio sits down next to Madeline, her best friend.

"Why are you wearing such a ridiculous costume?" Madeline whispers. "Halloween is six months away!"

"This is not a costume," Princess Pistachio proudly states. "I *am* a princess. A real princess. I am Princess Pistachio of Papua!"

Princess Pistachio's former best friend begins to giggle uncontrollably.

Madeline giggles so hard that
she does not see Mrs. Trumpethead's
menacing shadow looming over her
desk. Madeline spends the rest of class in
the hallway.

At recess, Princess Pistachio makes a
beeline for Madeline, angry as can be.

"How dare you laugh at me?"

"Pistachio Shoelace! Look at yourself! You are no more a princess than I am. What has got into you? Has a charming prince begged you to try on a glass slipper? Have toads asked you to kiss them?"

"Hummmpf!" Princess Pistachio sneers. "You are jealous. It is clear to me that you do not have a single drop of royal blood in your veins. You—"

Madeline bursts into laughter.

"Princess Pi-Pi-Pistachio of Pa-Pa-Papua! Ha, ha, ha!"

Princess Pistachio whips around and walks away, head held high, a proud smile on her face. But suddenly she trips over her dress, spins around twice, and lands in a huge mud puddle!

All the kids laugh.

Red as a tomato, black with mud, Princess Pistachio wants to cry.

"A princess never cries," she reminds herself and clenches her jaw. "Never, never!"

Fortunately, the recess bell rings.

After her endless day at school, Princess Pistachio slowly makes her way back home. Her beautiful princess dress is covered in mud and clings to her bum. Her crown gives her a headache, and her heart is as heavy as a storm cloud.

Madeline and Chichi speed past her on their skateboards.

"Hey, Pistachio!" Madeline jeers. "How many toads did you kiss today? Ha, ha, ha!"

"Where is your golden carriage?" Chichi teases. "Did it turn into a pumpkin? Ha, ha, ha!"

Princess Pistachio clenches her fists, but does not even look at them. She makes herself a promise—she will show those pumpkin-heads that she is a real princess. Oh, yes, indeed! Her friends will dearly regret making fun of her!

But *how* can she show them?

· Chapter 4 ·
A Princess of Nothing at All

The phone rings as Princess Pistachio walks into her house.

It is her grandfather.

"Hello, my little princess," he says. "Did you receive my present?"

Silence.

"Pistachio?"

"Grandpa?" Princess Pistachio asks in a very small voice. "You...you were the one who sent the crown? You were the one who wrote the card?"

"Yes," her grandfather answers. "But I think I forgot to sign it. Does the crown fit you? Do you like it?"

"It is a wonderful crown," Pistachio replies in an even smaller voice. "Thank you, Grandpa."

"Nothing is too beautiful for my favorite little princess," her grandfather adds. Pistachio hangs up.

Her heart sinks.

She is not a princess.

They were right. She is nothing at all.

Pistachio stares sadly out the window.
Out of the corner of her eye, she sees
Penny and the dog splashing about in
the paddling pool.

Oh no! Pistachio is horrified. She cannot
believe her eyes. The dog is wearing her
favorite purple blouse and her beautiful red
beret! Penny is washing the dog with her
magnificent leopard-print scarf!

Pistachio explodes.

She storms out of the house and howls, "PENNEEEY!" She rips the scarf out of her sister's hands. She undresses the dog at full speed.

"The dog is a pwincess!" Penny begins to cry.

"The dog is *not* a princess!" Pistachio rages. "You are *not* a princess! I am the ONLY princess here!"

Pistachio flies up the stairs, slams her bedroom door behind her, and throws herself onto the bed.

"I wish…I wish…Penny would disappear forever!" she cries.

Finally Pistachio falls asleep, her heart as tight as her fists.

• Chapter 5 •
A Princess in the Dark

It is almost nighttime when Pistachio's father wakes her up.

"Pistachio, is Penny in your room?"

"Of course not," Pistachio says sleepily. "She is not even allowed in here."

"She has disappeared," her father continues. "She was playing with the dog out front...and suddenly she was gone!"

Pistachio blushes. She knows what has happened.

Her wish was granted!

Pistachio jumps out of bed. She must find her sister.

Night has fallen. The whole neighborhood is looking for Penny. Flashlight beams streak across the dark sky like great white ribbons. Worried voices call, "Penny! Penneeey!"

Penny is nowhere to be found.

Pistachio looks all over the house—
under the beds, in the cupboards, in the
bottom of every sock drawer, behind the
fridge, in the fridge, in the attic, in the
basement. Everywhere!

No Penny.

Pistachio searches the garden. She is alone. It is as dark as a wolf's den. Her father's tomatoes make faces and whisper to each other. The cauliflowers try to trip her up. Thorny rosebushes grab at her legs.

"A real princess is brave." Pistachio shivers with fear. "I am not very brave, but I have to find Penny. It is my fault that she has disappeared."

Suddenly, a strange noise makes her jump. A loud rumbling growl. It sounds like a snoring dragon. The sound is coming from the far edge of the garden, where the darkest shadows dance.

"Could a d-d-dragon have eaten Penny?" Pistachio wonders as she tiptoes towards the sound. Her hand shakes and her flashlight flickers on and off. The closer she gets to the shadows, the louder the noise becomes. Now it sounds like an entire family of dragons snoring away.

Pistachio fumbles about, trips over some giant roots, and stumbles against the garden shed. She peeks inside.

Penny and the dog are snuggled close together. They are snoring loud enough to wake up any sleeping dragons.

"*Penny*," Pistachio whispers.

Penny opens her eyes. She smiles.
Pistachio holds out her hand.

"Come, Princess Penny. Time to go
home."

Princess Pistachio
and the Pest

Translated by Jacob Homel

To my friend Lucie Papineau

• Chapter 1 •
A Bad Start
to Summer Vacation

"Pistachio Shoelace!" Mrs. Trumpethead shouts. "Are you listening to me?"

Pistachio is startled. Mrs. Trumpethead's face looms over her. Her eyes shoot lightning. Her eyebrows are small, slimy black vipers.

"Y-y-yes, Mrs. T-t-Trumpethead," Pistachio stutters.

"Then answer my question!" Her teacher hollers.

Her black vipers gather at her brow in a V.

"What is two plus two?"

Total silence. You could have heard a tadpole diving. A fly flying. Pistachio, desperate, thinks as hard as she can.

"Um...," she mutters.

A few children start laughing.

"Two plus two?" Mrs. Trumpethead roars.

"Five?" mumbles Pistachio.

Half the class bursts into laughter.

"Six?" she whispers.

The entire class is rolling on the floor.

"TWO PLUS TWO!" bellows Mrs. Trumpethead.

Her black vipers wriggle and squirm. Her nostrils flare. A real dragon.

"Four! Four! Four!" Pistachio screams, but her teacher cannot hear her.

Pistachio wakes up, screaming, in her bed. The dog is gently licking her cheek. Sunlight floods her room.

"Phew!" she breathes out. "What a nightmare!"

And just then, Pistachio remembers that it is the start of summer vacation!

"Hurray!" she shouts, jumping out of bed. "Hurray! No more school! No more mean old Trumpethead! No more homework! Time for adventures and freedom! Hurray!"

Pistachio throws her clothes on. No
crown for her this morning. She slaps
on her baseball cap, takes her backpack
and her flashlight, and careens down the
stairs. She rushes into the kitchen like
a tornado. She's singing loud enough
to rattle the windows. Loud enough to
wake the neighbors.

"No more pencils, no more books, no
more teachers'—"

"My princess…," her mother stops her.

Her voice is too soft. Her maple syrup tone. Pistachio looks up at her mother with suspicion. But her mother is smiling at her. A smile that would melt a snowman in winter.

"My princess," she says again, "could you take your sister to the park this morning? I've got work to finish. Please?"

Pistachio's heart falls to her belly button.

"No way!" she says. "It is the first day of summer vacation—and I am supposed to meet up with Madeline and Chichi— we're going to explore the cavern down at the cemetery—and then—"

"Pistachio," her mother says, "I need your help."

There is no more maple syrup in that voice.

"No fair!" Pistachio protests. "I am going to die of boredom with her—"

Her mother is no longer smiling. A cold gust of wind blows through the kitchen.

"I go park!" Penny shouts, "With Pish-tasho!"

"Oh, no," Pistachio sighs, discouraged.

"Oh, yes!" her mother says. "I am sure you are going to have all sorts of fun. Right, Penny?"

Penny's smile reaches both her earlobes. She has squashed banana in her hair, on her nose, and even in her ears.

"Eeeeew!" Pistachio says.

• Chapter 2 •
A Little Thief

Half an hour later, Pistachio hits the road. She is dragging behind her the wagon piled high with dolls, stuffed animals, plastic buckets, shovels, rakes, and…her little sister! Penny wears her rabbit-ear hat and her Superman cape. She looks ecstatic. She has also managed to hide the dog under a stuffed elephant.

"Did you have to bring every single toy you own?" Pistachio grumbles, out of breath. "I feel like a work horse."

"Gee up, Pish-tasho! Gallop, gallop, Pish-tasho!"

And here come Madeline and Chichi on their bicycles. When they see Pistachio, they brake, their tires screeching. The wagon disappears in a cloud of dust.

"Hey, Pistachio!" Madeline says, "Are you coming with us to explore the cavern down at the cemetery? We have candles and a compass."

"No," Pistachio mutters. "I have to take my sister to the park."

"What?" Chichi sneers. "You prefer playing dolly with a baby?"

Madeline and Chichi zoom off, laughing like monkeys.

"But…but…," Pistachio begins.

Too late though. They are already far away.

"Rats! It's not fair! My friends get to have great adventures, and I have to spend all my time with a baby."

"I not baby! I Super-Rabbit!" Penny
shouts.

"Yeah, right, sure…," Pistachio
mutters, rolling her eyes. "I Tarzan, you
Super-Rabbit!"

Under a burning sun, Pistachio walks
slowly. Behind her, perched on the
mountain of toys, Penny sings, "Giddy
up, Giddy up, Giddy up up up!" at the
top of her voice.

The dog is snoring. Pistachio is daydreaming about exploring the cemetery's cavern. It is dark and silent. Suddenly, a rustling, a whisper: bats are brushing past her with their humid wings. She almost jumps out of her skin when she hears a growling voice coming from behind her.

"Stop! You! Stop right there, you little thief!" shouts Mr. Pomodoro, the local grocer.

He is as red as a tomato. He looks furious.

"Are you not ashamed! What a bad example for your *piccola* sister!"

"What? What's going on?" Pistachio replies, flabbergasted.

A small crowd appears around them. People are whispering and pointing fingers at her!

"And what's-a-more, you pretend to be innocent! *Mamma mia!*" Mr. Pomodoro says.

He digs his two arms in the pyramid of toys and dolls. He wakes up the dog, who, surprised, begins to bark.

"And this, what is this?" the grocer asks, brandishing two bananas.

Pistachio's eyes go as wide as saucers.

"And this? This is a beach ball, maybe?"

He puts a melon under her nose. The crowd laughs. The dog barks even louder.

"But, but… where does it all come from?" Pistachio asks, a bit dazed by the brouhaha.

"From my stand! *Mamma Mia!* If I ever I catch you again, you little good-for-nothing, I'll call the *polizia!*"

On that note, he turns and walks toward his shop, head held high. The crowd disperses, muttering.

"What a disgrace!" The baker says. "But who is the little thief?"

"Pistachio Shoelace!" Abraham replies, sneering. "She is in my class."

"Ah! Kids these days!" sighs an old man. "When I was young, these sorts of things never happened!"

Pistachio stands there, like a statue, her mouth open and her cheeks burning red. She does not understand any of it. Then she sees her sister sneak a pear from underneath the stuffed goat. She takes a big bite from it.

Pistachio finally understands. Penny is the thief! She is the little good-for-nothing, not Pistachio! Anger rises in her like a strong wind, hot and red. She grabs the pear out of her sister's hands and hurls it into the street. *SPLAT!* A car squashes it like a pancake.

Penny howls, furious.

Pistachio's eyes are stormy black and her teeth are clenched. She sets off for the park again, pulling behind her a sulking rabbit, its ears flapping sadly. The dog follows them from far behind, his tongue hanging like a pink sock.

· Chapter 3 ·
Oldtooth the Witch

Pistachio finally sees the park's entrance at the end of the deserted street. All of a sudden she spies her friend Rachid rollerblading toward her, bent under the weight of his large backpack.

"Ho! Pistachio! Are you coming to explore the cavern at the cemetery? I hear there is an amazing treasure right down at the bottom. I have a pickaxe and a shovel. Madeline and Chichi are bringing—"

"—Candles and a compass. I know, I know," Pistachio sighs, "but I can't go. I have to—"

"Take your dolls for a walk?" Rachid interrupts, laughing.

"I am bringing my sister and HER dolls to the park, can't you see?"

"Your invisible sister, I am guessing?" Rachid adds.

"My sister is invis...?"

Pistachio turns around. The dolls and stuffed animals are looking back at her with a stunned air. But where is Penny?

"Have fun, Pistachio!" Rachid calls out, then he vanishes in the blink of an eye.

Pistachio, in a panic, looks from one
end of the street to the other. Empty!

"Find Penny!" she tells the dog.

The dog turns around, nose to the
ground, ears flapping in the wind.
Pistachio follows him closely. Suddenly
the animal stops in front of a stone wall,
one leg in the air.

"Pish-tasho! Pish-tasho!" A squeaky
voice calls out.

It is Penny, perched all the way up on
top of the wall, like a bird on a wire.

"Don't move!" Pistachio says.

"I Super-Rabbit," Penny shouts. "I fly!"

She swirls her cape and prepares to jump into the air.

"NOOOOOOOOO!" Pistachio howls.

Penny, surprised, falls…on the other side of the wall. Pistachio hears a soft cry. Then, total silence.

Panicked, Pistachio climbs the wall. The old mossy stones are slippery. She breaks her nails and scratches her knees. Pistachio carefully peeks over the wall and sees Penny lying flat on her stomach in a sea of red flowers. She is as still as a mouse.

Oh, no! Pistachio thinks. She jumps down into the garden and runs to her little sister.

"Penny?" she whispers.

No answer. Maybe her sister is
seriously wounded? Maybe she is dead?
Pistachio is afraid. Suddenly, Penny
jumps up and bellows, "Surprise! I
Super-Rabbit!"

She bursts into laughter and falls back
into the flowers. Red petals swirl in the air.

Pistachio is both very relieved and
very angry.

"You bird brain!" She shouts. "Wait
until I—"

"What are you doing in my garden?"
A loud, creaky voice complains. "You
little pesky pests. You have come to cause
trouble, I know!"

Pistachio turns with horror to see Mrs.
Oldtooth approaching them, holding
herself up with her bent cane. Small, fat,
and hunchbacked, she hides her nasty
old face under a large black felt hat.
All of the neighborhood kids know her.
Everyone calls her Oldtooth the Witch.

"I would not mind turning you both into toads," Mrs. Oldtooth grumbles.

"I hungwy!" Penny shouts.

Her rabbit ears waggle over the flowers.

"Hush!" Pistachio says between clenched teeth, "do not be scared!"

"I not scawed!" Penny shouts. "I hungwy!"

"I am hungry as well," Mrs. Oldtooth growls, "I would not mind chomping on a bit of plump rabbit. Yum-yum!"

She hobbles closer, one hand digging in her huge hairy handbag.

"Yes, yes, a nice rabbit stew. That would not be bad at all. With a warm toad soup—oh, just delicious! Well, now! Where did I put my magic wand?"

Mrs. Oldtooth puts her handbag on the ground and sticks her whole head into it, searching for her wand.

"You little pests," she says, her voice muffled, "just you wait and see!"

Pistachio takes advantage of
Oldtooth's distraction. She grabs Penny
and carries her under her arm like
a small sack of potatoes. She starts
running toward the wall.

"You will never get me, you old
witch!" Pistachio hollers.

And just like that, she climbs over the
wall and disappears on the other side.

Mrs. Oldtooth takes her head out of
her bag and looks up. She smiles.

"Works every time," she says.

Her creaky laugh echoes in the empty
street.

• Chapter 4 •
Pistachio's Treasure

Finally, they are at the park. Pistachio sets Penny down in the sandbox with her bucket, her shovels, and her stuffed animals. Pistachio collapses on a bench under the shadow of a tree and wipes her forehead. *Whew! That was close!* she thinks.

As she is catching her breath, she starts daydreaming again of the cavern in the cemetery.

If only she could explore it… She
would be the one to find the hidden
treasure. She is sure of it! She sees
herself crawling in a narrow and humid
tunnel, a candle in her hand. All of a
sudden, she sees a glowing light. No,
two! The eyes of the dragon, guardian
of the treasure. He is lying on a pile of
gemstones, jewels, and gold coins. The
dragon opens his smoking maw wide
and howls—

"Pish-tasho! Pish-taaaa-sho!"

Pistachio jumps up. She turns around and sees Penny swimming in the fountain's basin. Suddenly her sister dives, splashing all the pigeons. SPLASH! You can only see her stripy socks. She reappears immediately, a big smile on her face.

"Pish-tasho!" she shouts. "Come see!"

Pistachio is furious. What a pest! She runs to the fountain.

"Penny! That's enough! Get out of there right now!"

"I found a tweasure!" Penny shouts.

A treasure? Pistachio comes nearer. Penny places a handful of coins on the side of the fountain. She smiles proudly.

Pistachio clenches her jaw and tells her sister, "You fish head! That is not a treasure. People throw coins in the basin to make a wish. It is forbidden to take them out."

"That is exactly right!" a serious voice says.

It is the park warden.

"It is also prohibited to swim in the fountain, prohibited to walk on the grass, prohibited to bring animals without a leash," he continues.

"Those are stuffed animals!" Pistachio protests.

From the corner of her eye, she sees that the dog is hiding behind a tree.

The man takes a small black book from his pocket and reads out loud.

"Article 213, paragraph b): *It is strictly prohibited to bring any animal (stuffed or alive) without a leash to the park.* There!" He says, satisfied. "Now, get out of my park. Miss, you should be ashamed of yourself, forcing this sweet little girl to dive into the fountain to find money for you."

"But, but…," Pistachio stammers.

"No buts! Get out!"

The warden places his black book in his pocket and crosses his arms. Pistachio grabs her dripping sister, who is flopping about like a fish, and places her back in the wagon.

She leaves, head down, under the furious stare of the park warden. Penny, all smiles, waves at him. The dog follows them like a shadow, hiding behind tree after tree.

The two sisters finally get back home around noon. Pistachio, red and breathless, pulls behind her a very damp and wrinkled Super-Rabbit.

"So?" Their mother asks. "Did you have fun?"

"Pheeew!" Pistachio sighs. "Thanks to Penny, I was accused of theft, then I was almost turned into a toad, and, worst of all, we were kicked out of the park. I am done! I am not going to take care of this brainless baby anymore."

"Not baby," Penny shouts, "I Super-Rabbit!"

"What amazing adventures!" her mother says. "I have the impression that you were not bored for a second, my princess, right?"

Pistachio stares at her mother. *On what planet does she live?* she thinks. *She doesn't understand anything!*

"But on the other hand, maybe it is too much for you. Tomorrow, I will ask a neighbor to come and keep an eye on you both."

"Who?" asks Pistachio, curious.

"You know her: dear, sweet Mrs. Oldtooth."

"Oh, no!" the two sisters shout in unison.

Pistachio immediately says, "Don't worry, Mom. I will take care of Penny tomorrow. I am sure we will have fun. Right, Penny?"

"Yes!" cries Penny. "You Tarzan, me Suuuuper-Rabbit!"

Princess Pistachio
and Maurice the Magnificent

For Jacob

Chapter 1

A Dog's Life

Princess Pistachio's dog is sleeping belly-up on his favorite plaid cushion. He is snoring like a frog with a cold. Every few seconds, his short legs spin frantically in the air as if he were swimming upside down. He whimpers and drools.

I wonder what he dreams about, thinks Pistachio. *Running after squirrels? Being a superhero? Winning a dog marathon?*

Her dog sleeps most of the day. Then he sleeps most of the night. In between naps, he eats.

A dog's life is really boring, thinks Pistachio. *Poor Dog. He needs adventure and excitement in his life.*

"Dog, let's go for a walk," says Pistachio. "A nice long walk in the park."

Dog rolls over.

"Let's play ball!" says Pistachio. She bounces his ball on the floor.

Dog snorts. Pistachio opens the door. Dog opens one eye.

"Come on, Dog." Pistachio is growing impatient.

Dog grunts as he heaves himself up onto his tiny legs. He waddles to the door. He looks outside. He sighs, shakes his head, and waddles back to his cushion.

Minutes later, he is snoring like a small train engine. Pistachio rolls her eyes.

Things have got to change around here, she thinks. *Dog will die of boredom.*

The next morning, Pistachio stuffs an astonished Dog into her schoolbag.

"School is sometimes boring too, but you might learn something new," says Pistachio. "Like reading or geography. Wouldn't that be exciting?"

Dog stares at her from the bottom of the schoolbag. He doesn't seem very excited.

Penny, who has been spying on Pistachio from beneath the bed, yells, "Wanna go school wif Dog!"

"Shhhhh, Penny! I'll bring you to school tomorrow," Pistachio lies.

"Wanna go NOW!" Penny roars.

Pistachio hears her mother coming up the stairs. She has to act fast.

"Here, Penny, you can wear my princess crown!"

Penny stops crying. She crawls out from under the bed. She is covered in dustballs.

"Weally?" She puts the crown on. It covers half her face.

"I better be going," says Pistachio as she shoulders her enormous schoolbag.

"What do you have in there?" asks her mother as Pistachio runs down the stairs. "It looks awfully heavy."

"Mr. Grumblebrain gave us a ton of homework," mutters Pistachio. "As usual." She runs out the door.

"Have a good day, princess!" calls her mother.

Rats! Pistachio has forgotten that it's Show and Tell at school today.

First, Chichi presents his favorite paper clip. He shows the class how he can twist it like a pretzel. Mr. Grumblebrain is not impressed.

Then, Fatima, the teacher's pet, presents her butterfly collection. She gives the Latin name to every single one: *Danaus plexippus, Zerene eurydice, Lycaeides melissa melissa*— Most of the students fall asleep.

"Verrrrrry interesting, Miss Fatima," says Mr. Grumblebrain. "Your turn, Miss Pistachio."

Pistachio peeks into her schoolbag. She has no choice. She will have to present her dog for Show and Tell.

"Come on out, Dog," whispers Pistachio. Dog snorts.

"Is someone blowing their nose in your schoolbag?" asks Sebastian. Everybody giggles.

"Dog," says Pistachio. "Wake up!"

Pistachio dumps her schoolbag on Mr. Grumblebrain's desk. Dog flops out like a pile of laundry. He shakes his head. His ears flap like clothes on a line. A stack of exam papers flutter to the floor. Dog sniffs Mr. Grumblebrain's apple and licks it. Then he swallows an eraser in one gulp. He stretches out on the desk and promptly falls asleep again.

By this time, the class is roaring with laughter. Elliot is the first to throw his eraser at the dog. He is not the last.

"Get that hairy beast off my desk!" yells Mr. Grumblebrain. "NOW!"

Pistachio, her face as red as a tomato, stuffs Dog back in her schoolbag, and, head held high, walks to her desk. She sits and stares straight ahead, wishing she were invisible. Or instantly transported to a desert island. Or both.

• Chapter 2 •
The Audition

Two days later, Pistachio is walking back from school with Madeline, her best friend, when she spots a sign posted in the window of the bookstore.

WANTED

Talented, intelligent, beautiful dog to play starring role in a theater production. Only serious dogs need apply. Call 321-B-A-R-K for an audition.

Management, Doggone Theater

Fireworks go off in Pistachio's mind.
"That's it!" she cries.

"What are you talking about?" says
Madeline.

"Read that," says Pistachio. "That's
the perfect job for Dog!"

Madeline reads the sign. At first, she
smiles. Then she starts giggling. Then she
roars with laughter.

"You've got to be kidding," she gasps, tears streaming down her face.

"What? What's so funny?" asks Pistachio.

"Can't you read?" says Madeline. "It says, 'Wanted…talented, intelligent, beautiful dog.' Hahaha!"

"So?" says Pistachio impatiently.

"Your dog is a fat ball of fur," says Madeline, "with a brain the size of a green pea."

"How can you say that?" shouts Pistachio, "Dog has many hidden talents."

"Like snoring?" asks Madeline. "Like eating erasers? Like sleeping all day?"

"He needs his beauty sleep," says Pistachio. "And, anyway, you don't know anything about dogs."

"Pistachio Shoelace!" says Madeline.

"Your dog couldn't ever, ever in a million, trillion years, star in a show. He has nothing between his tiny ears!" And Madeline skips away down the sidewalk.

Pistachio stands there, her cheeks burning like wildfire. "I'll show her," she says. "She'll eat her words."

The next day, Pistachio gets up early and washes and brushes Dog until his fur shines. She dresses him in his best dog collar. The bright purple one. They have a one o'clock audition at the Doggone Theater.

They are not alone. The place is
bursting with dogs and their proud
masters. Some dogs do double-somersaults.
Others juggle balls or shoes. A beagle
balances a teacup on her nose. Two
dachshunds do weird contortions.
They look like wrestling sausages. A
brown terrier tap-dances on a table. A
Chihuahua plays the trumpet.

Pistachio looks at Dog. He is sleeping
soundly at her feet. She sighs.

The dogs and their masters are called in one by one. Finally, it is their turn. Pistachio wakes Dog up and they pass through the small green door and onto the bare stage of a huge theater. The red velvet seats seem to climb up to the roof. Pistachio is blinded by the bright spotlights.

"Please take your places on the stage," says a deep voice that comes from nowhere. Pistachio squints into the dark theater. She can just make out a woman wearing thick glasses and sitting in the front row. She holds a clipboard in her hand. She is the theater director.

"No time to waste," says the woman. "Let's get this over with. I'm exhausted."

"What should we do?" asks Pistachio.

"Isn't it obvious? Go stand on the X and show me what your dog can do."

Pistachio gulps. Dog can't do much except find a ball. And that's only if it is hiding behind his bowl.

She walks to the center of the stage where a big X is chalked on the floor. "Dog, come here," she calls.

"Dog?" she calls again, a bit louder this time. *Where is he?*

The director sighs. "I don't have all day," she says. "You have only one minute left! Let's gogogo!"

"Dog?" whispers Pistachio, as she walks toward the green velvet curtain. "Come on, Dog. This is your big chance!"

Then her heart drops. She can hear
Dog snoring away. She pulls the curtain
back and there he is, sleeping like a
sloth, belly-up, his tiny legs waving in
the air.

Pistachio's shoulders droop. "Oooh,
Dog," groans Pistachio. She is so
disappointed.

The woman stands up. She adjusts her
glasses, peers at Dog, and smiles. "Hey!
This might be the one!" she exclaims.

"We are looking for a dog to play Sleeping Beauty."

Dog snores loudly.

"Brilliant!" says the director. "He's got the part!"

Pistachio's heart somersaults. She kneels down by Dog and hugs him tightly. "Oh, Dog," she whispers. "You are amazing!"

• Chapter 3 •
Stardom

"What's his name?" asks the director.

"Dog," says Pistachio. "Dog Shoelace."

"That won't do. He needs a stage name. A name for a star!"

She is right, thinks Pistachio. *Dog is going to have an exciting new life, so he needs an exciting new name.*

That evening, Pistachio looks up words in the dictionary. She tries them out on Dog.

"Frederic the Fantastic?" says Pistachio. Dog rolls his eyes.

"Astounding Antonio?" says Pistachio. Dog sighs.

"Stupendous Stirling?" says Pistachio.

Dog puts his head on his paws and closes his eyes.

It is Pistachio's turn to sigh. Then she thinks of her grandfather.

His name is Maurice.

"Maurice?" she whispers. "Maurice the Magnificent?"

Dog smiles in his sleep.

Life becomes a whirlwind for Pistachio and Maurice the Magnificent. There are rehearsals every day

after school. Maurice practices sleeping for hours on end. There are costume fittings. There are appointments with the manicurist, who paints his nails a lovely shade of peony pink, and the *coiffeur,* who curls the hair between his ears. Pistachio and Maurice are interviewed over and over by the press. They want to know every single detail of Maurice's life. When did he start dreaming of being an actor? What is his favorite color? What does he like to eat? Does he have a secret love?

Life is definitely not boring anymore.

Pistachio invites her family and her friends to the opening night. Even Madeline is there. They all sit together in the front row. As soon as the curtains are drawn, the audience falls silent. They are hypnotized by Maurice's performance. No one has ever seen an actor sleep or snore with such flair.

The play is an astounding success. When Maurice comes out to bow, he gets a standing ovation. Only Madeline stays seated.

Maurice the Magnificent is a star!
The show is extended for six months.
Maurice has his own dressing room. It is
filled with flowers and fresh bones.

His fans wait for him every night at

the back door of the theater. Poodles
faint. Beagles throw kibble at him.
His face is on the first page of every
newspaper in the country.

Pistachio is so proud. All she can
talk about is Maurice…*Maurice did this,
Maurice did that, Maurice is…*

"That's enough! Stop talking about Maurice!" says Madeline one day. "I can't stand it anymore!"

Pistachio sniffs. "You're just totally jealous, Madeline Maplehead! You desperately wish you had a wonderful world-famous dog like Maurice!"

"Jealous," says Madeline, "of a fat furball? You must be kidding." She snickers loudly and walks away. As soon as Madeline turns the corner, she frowns and her shoulders droop. She looks like she has lost something precious.

• Chapter 4 •
Dognapping

But then, one terrible day, Pistachio goes backstage to Maurice's dressing room after the show.

"Maurice!" calls Pistachio. "It is time to go home." She enters the dressing room. It is empty. A ruby dog collar lies on the floor. A half-chewed bone is abandoned on a cushion.

Suddenly, Pistachio's throat is as dry as sandpaper. She knows something is wrong.

"Maurice!" she cries. "Where are you?" She looks under the couch. In the top drawer of the dresser. In the closet. Then she sees the note taped to the mirror.

Pistachio's heart stands still. Maurice
has been dognapped!

As Pistachio slowly walks home, her mind is racing. *What should I do? If I call the police, the dognapper might hurt Maurice. Should I pay the ransom? What if the dognapper keeps Maurice a prisoner forever?*

Suddenly, Pistachio sees Madeline swinging like a monkey from a tree branch. She seems to be waiting for Pistachio.

"So, where is the world-famous furball?" asks Madeline, "Did he fall off the stage?"

Pistachio tells her the whole, terrible story. She is almost in tears.

"What should I do, Madeline? You are my best friend. Please help me."

"Why would I want to help you?" Madeline asks. "I don't feel like I am your best friend anymore."

Madeline swings back and forth. Pistachio walks away.

Pistachio makes up her mind. She
will trick the dognapper. She will save
Maurice.

That night at nine o'clock, Pistachio
sneaks out of the house. She runs all the
way to the park. She places an envelope
at the foot of the chestnut tree. Then
she looks around to make sure that no
one is there. She scrambles up the tree
and settles on a big branch. An owl
hoots and sails off into the dark velvet
night. Pistachio waits. She doesn't move
an inch.

At exactly ten o'clock, a shadow
creeps silently toward the foot of the tree.
Pistachio holds her breath.

The shadow grabs the envelope and
snickers. Pistachio jumps down from
the branch. She lands on the shadow.
The shadow shrieks. Pistachio shines her
flashlight in the shadow's face.

"Madeline?" cries Pistachio. "*You* are
the dognapper?"

Just then, a fat, furry ball flies into Pistachio's arms and nearly licks her face off.

"Why did you steal Maurice?" asks Pistachio.

"You were right," answers Madeline miserably. "I *was* jealous. Terribly jealous. I wanted to be your best friend again. You only had eyes for Maurice. I felt so lonely. I'm sorry."

Pistachio is silent for a moment. Had she really forgotten all about her friend? Maybe she had.

"How about if the three of us become best friends?" says Pistachio. "You, Maurice, and I."

"Okay," says Madeline. "But can you and Maurice get off of me first? You are both pretty heavy."

Maurice the Magnificent decided that he had had enough excitement and that it was time to retire. He needed to catch up on his sleep.

Pistachio and Madeline went on to start a school for dog-actors.

Dog Stars!
Do you want your dog to become a star?
Does your dog have any talent?
Find out at Dog Stars!
Call Madeline or Pistachio
444-STAR